by *Jillian Powell*
Illustrated by **Mark Penman**

Titles in the Full Flight Thrills and Spills series:

The Knight Olympics	Jonny Zucker
Pied Piper of London	Danny Pearson
The Science Project	Jane A C West
Gorilla Thriller	Richard Taylor
Clone Zone	Jillian Powell
Clowning Around	Helen Orme
Time to go Home	David Orme
Haunted Car	Roger Hurn
Dinosaur Rampage	Craig Allen
Rubbish Ghost	Jillian Powell

Badger Publishing Limited
Suite G08, Stevenage,
Hertfordshire SG1 2DX
Telephone: 01438 791 037
Fax: 01438 791 036
www.badgerlearning.co.uk

Clone Zone ISBN 978-1-84926-983-4

Text © Jillian Powell 2013
Complete work © Badger Publishing Limited 2013

Publisher: Susan Ross
Senior Editor: Danny Pearson
Designer: Fiona Grant
Illustrator: Mark Penman

Printed and bound in China through Colorcraft Limited, Hong Kong

Contents

New words:

gadget	winked
detention	routine
sullen	rogue
hissed	batch
frown	clone

Main characters:

Lee

Max

Chapter 1

First Meeting

His ticket number flashed up on the screen. D002 was ready. Lee was in the Clone Zone.

Clones were the latest must-have gadget. To be cool, you had to have a clone: someone who looked and acted exactly like you. Lee was there to pick up his very own clone. He was not sure about this but his best mate Max already had one and he told Lee that clones were the best thing ever.

"Think of all the things you hate doing that you can get your clone to do!" he said.

So, Lee had thought about it. It didn't take long to come up with a list: double maths on Mondays, tidying his bedroom, getting a detention with Mr Hill, doing his English coursework… The list went on and on.

"There you go!" Max said. "And while your clone does all those horrible things, you can be out with your mates having fun, or playing on the games console."

"Or skateboarding!" Lee added. Maybe having a clone was not such a crazy idea, Lee thought.

"Exactly. What did I tell you? Clones are great. Everyone needs one!" Max said excitedly.

So here he was in the Clone Zone about to meet his own clone. It was an odd feeling. He handed over his ticket at the desk.

"Wait there," the man behind the desk said. When he came back, D002 was behind him.

Lee stared at his clone. It was almost like looking in a mirror.

"I'm Lee," he said. He held out his hand.

"I'm Lee," his clone said. The clone shook Lee's hand.

Back home, Lee had a pile of homework to do, or rather his clone did. Max was right, this was great!

Lee showed his clone where he was sleeping. "That's your bed," he told his clone. "It used to be mine but Mum got me this new bed."

His clone looked at the two beds then threw his bag onto Lee's new bed.

Maybe his clone had not heard him properly, Lee wondered.

"No, that one is yours," Lee said, throwing the bag across to the old bed.

"Tonight, we've got... I mean you've got some homework to do." Lee said. "I need to phone my mate Max. We've got a football match tomorrow and I need him to call me so I get up on time."

This was strange. His clone was just standing there staring at him.

"So, here are the maths books," Lee
said. "I've marked the pages you have
to do."

Lee put the books on his desk and his
clone sat down.

"Great. I'll be downstairs okay?"

His clone gave him a sullen look.

That look was a bit worrying. But then,
it was his clone, and that was just how
Lee looked when Mum told him to do
his homework!

Chapter 2

The Match

Lee was dreaming. He dreamed he was at the Clone Zone picking up his clone. But as they shook hands, another clone came out, then another. Suddenly, there were hundreds of Lee clones coming at him. He woke up with a start. No!

He looked at his watch. It was past ten o'clock. The football match had already started! Why hadn't Max called him like he said he would?

The other bed was empty. At least his clone was up. That was something. Lee had told him to get on with his history coursework.

He dressed, grabbed his football kit and rushed to the ground. He could see that they were about halfway through the match. Max was on the pitch, playing midfield.

"Oi!" why didn't you wake me?" Lee shouted to his friend. "I was looking forward to this match."

There was a sudden roar. One of their team had scored a goal. Lee looked down the pitch to see who had scored. It was his clone and he was wearing Lee's football kit!

"I thought that was you!" Max said. He was looking confused.

Lee was starting to feel angry.

"Well it's not. This is me, that's the clone. He should be at home doing history coursework!" Lee said crossly.

"Sorry mate. But look, he just scored a hat-trick," Max grinned. "Be honest, Lee. When was the last time you did that?"

Chapter 3

A Missed Date

The rest of the week at school was the same as the football match. Every time Lee planned on doing something, his clone got there before him.

Lee needed to do something. He was not putting up with this. He was going to have the fun, not his clone. There was a party on Friday night and Lee was keen to go. Amy was going to be there. He had liked her for ages.

There was no way his clone was going. Lee had to stop him, or rather, Mr Hill did. The idea came to Lee in Friday's break time.

He chatted non-stop through maths.
Mr Hill's face went red, then purple.
At last, he had had enough.

"That is it Lee, detention for you
tonight. See me there," Mr Hill shouted.

"But the party…" Max hissed from
behind. Lee turned round and winked
at him.

Lee stayed behind after school.
He made sure his clone was at the
detention room on time. He watched
Mr Hill follow him in. There was no
way his clone would get out with old
Hill there.

Max had already gone to the party
leaving his clone to tidy his room.

Lee packed up his school bag and made his way to the toilets. He wanted to try out a new hair gel. He had to look good for Amy.

On the way out, he sent Max a text:

'Is Amy there?'

His phone bleeped. He was about to read it when he heard someone shouting his name.

"Lee. Lee. Come back here!"

It was Mr Hill. His face was purple again. "What do you think you are doing?" he roared. "Get back in the detention room. You just got another hour of detention!"

Mr Hill frog-marched Lee back to the room. When they got there, his detention work was on the table. But the room was empty.

"I shall not be going out again and nor will you!" Mr Hill roared.

Lee sat, willing the time to pass. He might still make it to the party. But Mr Hill had other ideas. By the time Lee got out, it was too late.

Lee went straight home to his bedroom and lay on the bed. He read a text from Max. It said:

Gr8 party!
Result – U
got a date!

Chapter 4

A Discovery

The next day, Lee went to see Max. Max was playing on his games console. His clone was in the back, cleaning his football boots.

"Great party wasn't it?" Max grinned.

"Was it? I never made it!" Lee said crossly. "Can you believe it Max? He took my place again."

"He did?" Max was still looking at the console. He did not seem bothered by what Lee had just said.

"Did you hear me? My clone… He went to the party and I got the detention!" Lee repeated.

"Well you did play up in maths!" Max said.

"Yes, so he would get detention and I could go to the party… and meet Amy," Lee added.

"Well, you did get a date!" Max said.

"No I didn't, my clone did!" Lee snapped. What was the matter with Max? Why did he not get it?

"These clones are rubbish," Lee went on. "I'm fed up with mine already."

"I think clones are great, the best thing ever," Max told him. He nodded towards his clone.

Lee watched him. He was certainly cleaning the football boots well. Then Lee spotted something. The clone had earphones on, but he had them on the wrong way round. There was only one person who did that: Max. Would his clone do that too? Lee wondered.

Lee looked hard at Max, then back at his clone.

"Anyway, I want you to hear this track. It's cool," Lee said, pulling out his phone. He handed it over, with the earphones. Then he watched to see what Max would do next.

Max checked left and right on the earphones and carefully put them on… in the correct ears!

"Yeah, that's cool!" he agreed, nodding to the music.

Lee stared at him. Now he was sure. His mate Max was out in the back, cleaning football boots. So Lee was sure he was talking to Max's clone.

Max's phone rang. The clone rushed to answer it. Then Lee saw him frown and end the call.

What was going on here? Why was the real Max letting this happen? Lee had to find out… and fast.

Chapter 5

The Mix-up

When Lee got home, he had five missed calls. They were from the Clone Zone. There was a voicemail. It said:

This is the Clone Zone. WARNING: There are rogue clones at large. They must be sent back to the Zone at once for re-programming. These rogue clones are trying to take over lives.

REPEAT: Return them at once to the Zone.

So that was it! He knew it. Their clones were trying to take over. Lee had to get hold of Max – the real Max. He went to ring Max's mobile, then stopped.

The clone would answer. Instead, he rang Max's mum.

"He's out skateboarding," she told Lee.

"Is his clone there?" Max asked.

"Yes, he is catching up on Max's homework!" she said.

That would be the real Max then!

"Can I speak to him? He… needs to know something about our homework," Lee fibbed.

Lee explained everything to Max. Max sounded confused, like the clone had brainwashed him or something.

Lee told Max to meet him at the Clone Zone right away.

When he turned up, Max had still got his earphones on… the wrong way round. Great! It was the real Max.

"We need to get these clones sorted!" Lee told Max. Max was still not sure what was going on but he went along with Lee. He trusted his friend.

They went to the front desk.

"We are here about the rogue clones," Lee told the man at the desk.

The man nodded. He gave them forms to fill in and showed them into an empty room.

"We'd better get our clones here while we fill these in," Lee said.

They both sent a text home and told their clones to meet them at the Zone. They said it was for a routine check. Then they waited.

"It's like a prison in here," Max said. "They should get some pot plants or something."

"This is odd," Lee said as he filled in the form. "It says at the top 'Write Clone number here.'"

"I've done that!" Max said.

"Yes but look down the form," Lee said slowly. "It's not D.O.B. – date of birth, it's D.O.C – date of cloning."

The boys looked at each other.

These are the clones' forms," Max said. "They've given us the wrong forms!"

The room was deadly quiet. Suddenly, Lee jumped up. There was a small window in the door and he looked out.

"Hey, our clones are there, talking to the man at the desk!" he told Max. "Something is not right. We have to go and sort this out."

Just then a door opened on the other side of the room. Two men in doctors' coats came in.

"This way to re-programming please!" one of the men said coldly.

"Wait… you've got this wrong. We are not the clones!" Lee said.

"They are the clones out there!" Max said, pointing madly. He was just beginning to realise what was going on.

The men in coats looked at each other.

"This is what they do, try and take over. We better just ignore them," the other man said smiling.

"Just come with us and there won't be any trouble," they said, pushing the boys through the door...

Real-life Cloning

DOLLY THE SHEEP CLONED

22nd February 1997

Scientists in Scotland have announced the birth of the world's first cloned mammal, Dolly the sheep. They cloned a sheep by taking DNA from a single cell from its udder and implanting it into another sheep's egg cell, which had had its DNA removed. Dolly is the exact clone of the sheep that provided the DNA.

Did you know?

The first animal cloned was a tadpole in 1952. Dolly the sheep was the first mammal to be cloned. Scientists have cloned: goats, cows, mice, pigs, cats, dogs and rabbits. Since then, some people pay to have favourite pets cloned. Scientists have cloned human cells. Human cell clones can be used to research diseases like cancer and AIDS. Scientists are cloning human cells to try and grow organs that can be used to replace diseased organs.

Clones can suffer health problems and die early. Only one or two healthy lives result from every one hundred cloning experiments.

Some scientists want to try and create human clones but others argue this is wrong, and could be dangerous.

Questions about the Story

What is the first task Lee asks his clone to do?

What is the first sign that he has a rogue clone?

Why is Lee so keen to go to the party?

Why does Lee get an extra hour of detention?

What does Lee notice about Max's clone?

Why does Max happily do everything his clone should be doing?

What was the first animal ever to be cloned?

Would you clone yourself? If so why?